# TWO CAN PLAY

For Susan, thank you for all your advice,
pickles and rice pudding.

First published in Great Britain in 2021 by Andersen Press Ltd.,
20 Vauxhall Bridge Road, London, SW1V 2SA
Copyright © Margaret Sturton 2021.
The right of Margaret Sturton to be identified as the author and illustrator
of this work has been asserted by her in accordance with the
Copyright, Designs and Patents Act, 1988. All rights reserved.
Printed and bound in China.

1  3  5  7  9  10  8  6  4  2

British Cataloguing in Publication Data Available.
Hardback ISBN 978 1 78344 922 4
Paperback ISBN 978 1 78344 923 1

# TWO CAN PLAY

# MARGARET STURTON

Andersen Press

"What are you doing?" asked Puss.

"I'm planning our garden," said Cat.
"We'll need to work together to
make it magnificent. It'll be fun."

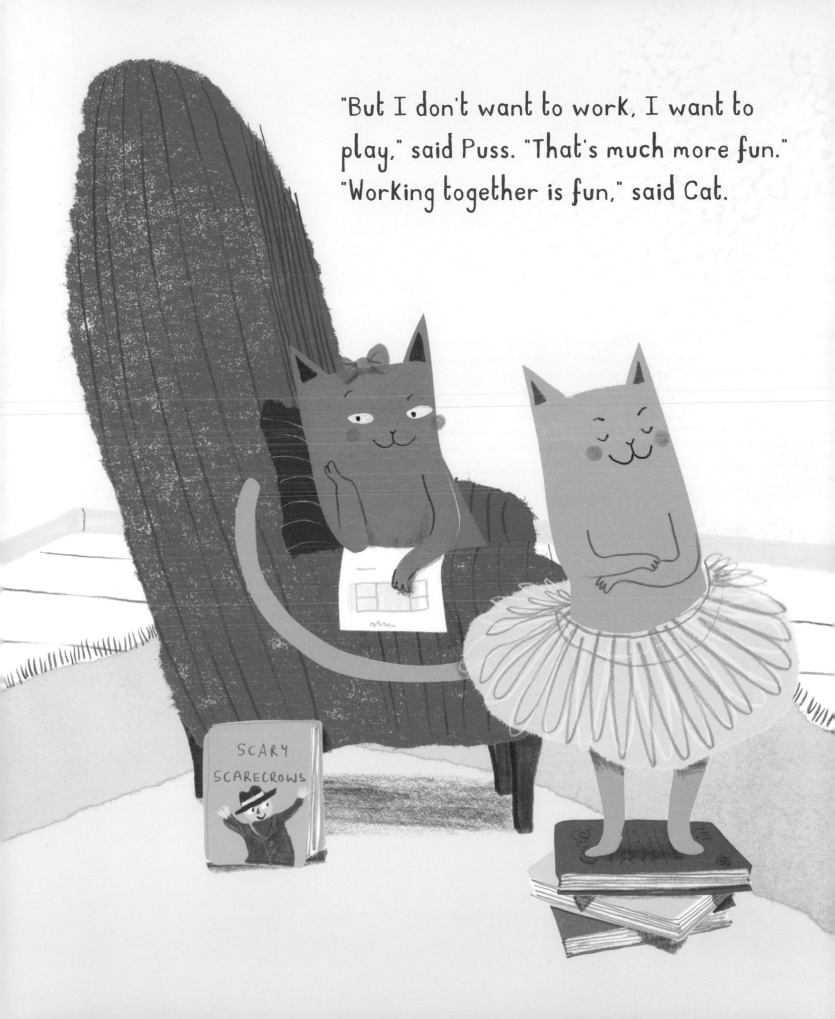

"But I don't want to work, I want to play," said Puss. "That's much more fun."
"Working together is fun," said Cat.

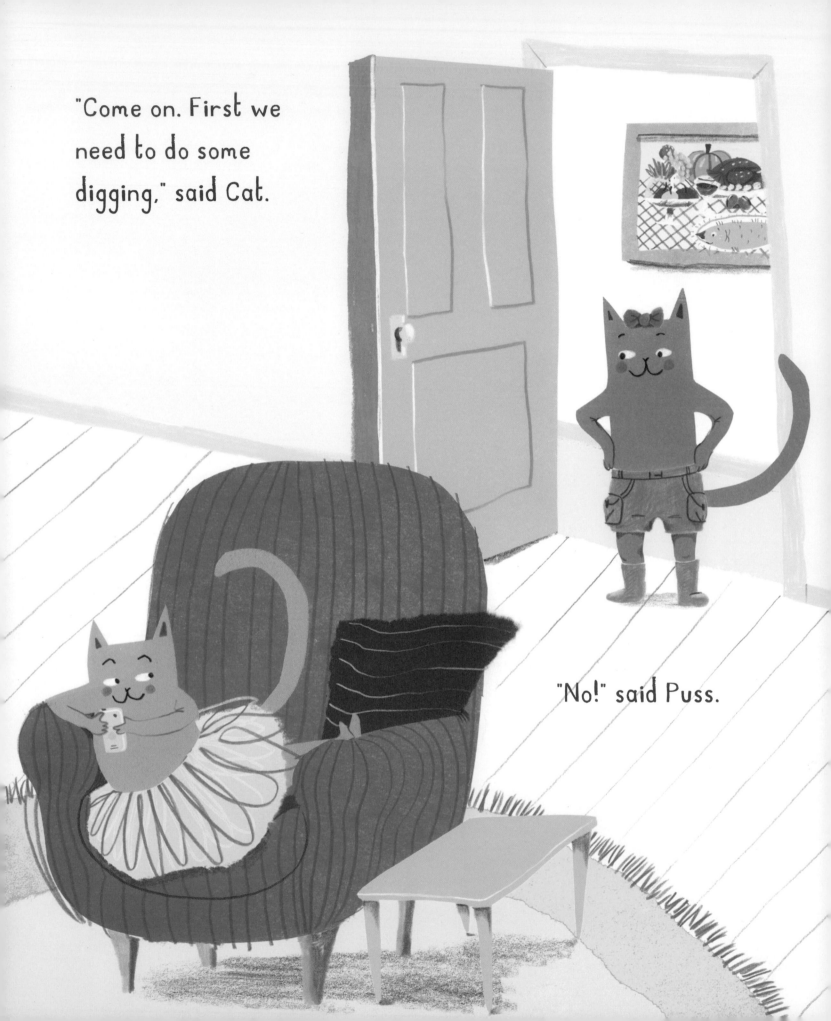

"Come on. First we need to do some digging," said Cat.

"No!" said Puss.

So Cat dug the garden by herself.

Puss thought digging looked like hard work.

"Will you come and choose some seeds?" asked Cat.

"No!" said Puss.

So Cat got herself ready...

and cycled into Town.

Cat chose the seeds she wanted.
Puss thought choosing seeds might actually
be a bit fun, but she would never say so.

"Will you help me plant the seeds?" asked Cat.

"No!" said Puss. "I told you, I just want to play!"

So Cat used her wheelbarrow
to collect what she needed...

and prepared the soil.

Cat planted the seeds
outside and waited for
her plants to grow.

Secretly, Puss liked watching plants grow too but she wasn't going to admit it.

"Will you help me scare the birds so they don't eat all the seedlings?" asked Cat.

"No!" said Puss, "That's not fun."

So Cat made model owls, chimes and mirrors that flashed in the sunlight.

Puss was tempted to join in.

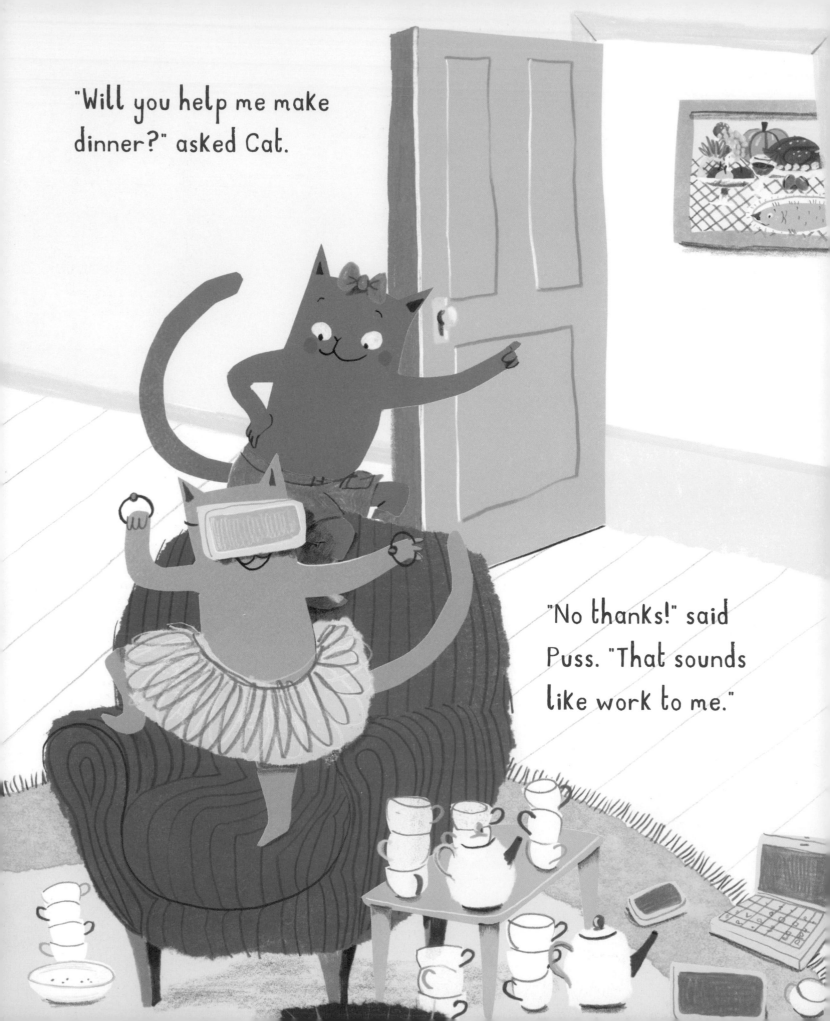

"Will you help me make dinner?" asked Cat.

"No thanks!" said Puss. "That sounds like work to me."

So Cat picked everything she needed to make a fine feast...

... and got to work in the kitchen. The cooking smells were wonderfully good.

"Please may I taste some?" purred Puss.

"Hmm..." said Cat.
"What do you think?"

"Perhaps... not," Puss said quietly, "because
I didn't do any of the work, did I?"

I'd better go and do
the washing-up."
Puss slowly walked
towards the kitchen.
"Hang on a minute,"
said Cat.

"Eating together is far more fun than eating alone.

So is playing while we do the washing-up.

And storing the extra fruit and vegetables for the winter together is the best fun of all!"

"You know, I've always thought
working together is the same as
playing and having fun," said Puss.
"Oh, really, is that so," said Cat.
"I wasn't expecting that."